CHRONICLES OF BADSHAPUR

PRINCE RAJVIR AND THE MAGICITY

RUSSELL RODRIGUES (LLESSUR)

Authors Note

The Chronicles of Badshapur (Emperors City) – fiction, are written for people young at heart and inquisitive of mind, specifically those who still believe in magical worlds filled with brave princes and pretty princesses, sly shape shifters and wise wizards, dangerous demons and deadly dragons

Synopsis

Book 1 – Prince Rajvir and the Magicity: A long time ago, in a land far away, a young Prince Rajvir sets out to the Magicity, to master his destiny under the guidance of the Grand Sorcerer Shahnawaz. Prince Rajvir is suddenly plucked from his carefree princely existence and thrust into a world of magic and illusion, danger and disaster which will help him prepare for his role as the future ruler of Badshapur.

Contents

Foreword

Table Of Contents

Chapter 1 – The Royal Family of Badshapur

Chapter 2 – Just another Princely Day

Chapter 3 – The Surprise

Chapter 4 – The Magicity

Chapter 5 – Flying High

Chapter 6 - Magical Moment Marathon

Chapter 7 – Sheep in Wolfs Clothing

Chapter 8 - The Enemy Within

Chapter 9 - The Beginning of the End

Prologue

Chapter 1 – The Royal Family of Badshapur

Prince Rajvir felt the suns rays shining in his face, woke up stretched and yawned. From the angle of the rays he realized it was 9.00 A.M. and he was late again for breakfast. His father Maharaja Shahvir Singh, would be displeased however his stepmother Maharani Kamini Devi would be extremely happy, and would get another opportunity to make him look bad albeit surreptitiously. Not that he cared anyway.

He sometimes wished that he was not born a Prince but could roam freely with his friends and do what he pleased , however since he was going to be King one day he would have to mind his manners and behave in a fashion that befit a Royal Prince of a 2000 year old dynasty. Tall, fair and muscular for his age, everyone said he looked like his mother – with large brown eyes, thick eyelashes and heavy brows. A long aquiline nose which flared into delicate nostrils like a thoroughbred, followed by full reddish lips, he could be mistaken for a girl if it wasn't for the manly cleft chin.

Prince Rajvir's mother had vanished from the royal gardens one day, when he was just 3 years old. All he could remember of her was that she was very beautiful, kind and gentle and had a very melodious voice, such that the birds would stop their singing to hear her. Rumor had it that the Gandharvas (fairy folk) had spirited her away so that she could sing for eternity in their golden courts.

Realizing that his young son would need a mother to take care of him – the Maharaja remarried a beautiful woman whom he came upon one dusk, while returning from a hunt in the forest. The moment she became Queen she immediately dismissed most of the old servants who were loyal to the Royal Family, brought her own entourage and acted like a doting mother in front of the King but she really couldn't care less about Rajvir's welfare, which she handed over to a Nurse who had a young son of her own. His Dai-Ma (Nurse) Avanti had taken care of him and protected him since.

Her son Krish became his dearest friend and they were inseparable.

The new Queen gradually started assisting the King in matters of state and he would not take any decisions without consulting her. Having lost one wife he did not wish to lose another and catered to her every whim and fancy, hoping she would equally love and care for his young son. After a few unsavory interactions with her, Prince Rajvir learned to stay out of her way which wasn't difficult considering her suite of rooms were in another wing of the palace – the Andher Kothi – Dark Rooms as the Sun's rays didn't reach there. She liked it that way. The Queen had requested the King that she needed some time to herself to pursue her own work and she spent that time in her tower suite. Only her faithful henchman Kalia (The Black One) was allowed in there and people said that strange muttering and rustling could be heard from behind the closed doors, but no one dared to question her as to how she spent her time, if they wanted to hold onto their heads.

Chapter 2 – Just another Princely Day

Rajvir jumped out of bed, completed his daily ablutions and howled for his nurse "DAIIIIII- MAAAAAA" like she was the last person in the world –which she was to him. As usual he couldn't find his clothes. The plump motherly woman bustled into the room and pulled his ear affectionately as she would her own son. "Naughty boy, do you know what the time is – yet you lie in bed for half the day" She smiled "I will tell Mandala(the court jester and storyteller) not to tell you anymore stories as you're then unable to sleep and hence unable to wake up on time. A fine King you'll make when you grow up.

"Noooo"shouted Rajvir-"I promise, I'll be good – please help me find my clothes, I've brushed my teeth, do I really need to also take a bath". "Yes, you better – else the Maharani will not let you sit at the table for breakfast. - I have heated water for you and filled your bathtub and told the cook to make your favorite breakfast – if you don't hurry, the Maharani will feed it to her pet dogs Rahu and Ketu

Prince Rajvir rushed into the bathroom, almost slipping on the mat and then jumped into the tub, merrily singing while bathing himself. Outside Avanti busied herself clearing his room, sighing when she saw the condition of his fine clothes spattered with clay from playing in the garden.

In 5 minutes he was done and rushed out in just a tiny towel and started changing his clothes. Avanti scolded him saying " You're no longer a baby, you're almost 12 years old – you should change in the bathroom- you're going to be King one day"

Prince Rajvir scowled, pulled on his Kurta and chudidar slipped on his sandals and rushed out the door , jumping down the stairs two @ a time , almost knocking down the old washer man who had come to collect the soiled linen. He gave a toothless smile and blessed the young prince. Prince Rajvir rushed into the dining room to find his father and the Queen still at breakfast. The King smiled to see his first born and then quickly frowned and looked pointedly at the Sundial in the center of the table, but one couldn't miss the twinkle in his eyes. The Queen pointedly commented "My dear son, it's good to see you're here finally for breakfast and earlier than yesterday" The 2 dogs near her feet growled and raised their hackles when they saw him, but the Queen quickly shushed them. There was no love lost between them and Prince Rajvir. Prince Rajvir surreptitiously stamped on Rahu's tail and kicked Ketu with his mojri (pointed shoe). Both howled and growled. The Queen glared at Prince Rajvir knowingly and said to herself "Daily the boy grows more and more insolent, he needs to be cut down to size"

Prince Rajvir quickly served himself and gobbled down the hot potato salad and Indian bread placed on his plate and gulped down his milk almost burning his tongue. In 10 minutes he was done and asked his father "Papaji can I leave now – I want to go find Krish so we can go to the stables. Rani the unicorn mare has given birth to a male colt that will be a fine stallion one day."

The king said "Son, what about your studies, when is Guruji (Teacher) meeting you today?" "Papaji" responded Prince Rajvir, "I won't be long – not more than half an hour – promise, will be back in a jiffy" and before his father could respond he was out the door "Hmmmm- the boy is becoming very irresponsible- he is no longer a child" said the Queen "I was just as carefree at his age "responded the King "I will have to personally supervise his studies" thought the King to himself.

Rajvir raced towards the royal stables almost falling over himself to see the new arrival. Manu the stable keeper was waiting for him and grinned to see the young prince. "Good Morning, your highness, you seem impatient, may I help you?" Rajvir asked "Where is he". Who "Krish?" asked Manu and winked. Rajvir frowned "You know whom I mean – the new foal" Oh, the foal, he is waiting for you Sire", and led the prince to the corner stable where Rani (the winged unicorn) was resting with the black foal. It had been a difficult labor and she hadn't completely recovered. The foal was coal black with a white spot on its forehead below its horn (like a cloud) and wonder of wonders its wings had white streaks like lightning. "I shall call him Badal" (Cloud) – thought Rajvir and shall fly him every day, once he has grown up, which won't be long. The foals sire could apparently be one of the wild flying unicorns who flew over the mountains at sunset to the highest peaks to feed on the tender buds and shoots and drink from the clearest mountain streams

(The winged unicorns grew much faster than normal horses and could be ridden within 3 months of being born)

Suddenly Manu and Prince Rajvir heard a murmur which increased in volume. They rushed outside and saw a group of villagers carrying an unconscious fisherman. Manu asked them what had transpired – they said that the fisherman had gone fishing in the enchanted lake and his boat had been pulled by the whirlpool in the middle – he had dived overboard and just managed to get to the shore before collapsing from exhaustion.

They laid him down and sprinkled water on his face- he came to and struggled and murmured "The voices are calling me, let me go"

The villagers started mumbling "It has begun again; at least we managed to save him, unlike the others"

What has begun again – asked Rajvir. Manu frowned and said "Nothing, just old wives' tales". It's almost noon, you need to get back to the castle and have your lunch."

Prince Rajvir grimaced and left – but he couldn't forget what had happened and wanted to get to the bottom of it.

As he was heading back, he bumped into Krish, who was coming from the opposite direction. "Where were you he asked"? Krish smiled and said "Looking for you". "You're such a liar" – you knew very well that we were supposed to see the foal today. "Sorry" said Krish "How is the foal".

"Very handsome "and he will be magnificent when he is older and I will ride him every day. "Lucky you "said Krish, enviously.

Krish, having grown up with little, appreciated whatever he received as gifts from the Prince but at times was torn within, seeing how Prince Rajvir took special things for granted.

His only plan once he grew up was to continue serving the Prince. He would happily continue to live in his little thatched cottage, get married to a pretty village girl to look after his mother.

His destiny was chalked out.

Chapter 3 – The Surprise

As he reached the palace Prince Rajvir heard Avanti calling for him – he rushed to her "Prince, where have you been the King wants to meet you urgently", he has something important to tell you. She made him have a wash and change his clothes. Prince Rajvir bore this and said "Dai-maa (Nurse Mother), can I go now"

She smiled, gave his hair a last brush and gave him a slight push "Go quickly"

The King was in the special courtroom adjoining the palace and his special courtiers were waiting. The doorman announced " His Highness Prince Rajvir " – Prince Rajvir walked in , bowed low before his father and sought permission to sit at the little couch below his father's throne where his step brother Prince Samir was sitting. The King frowned and beckoned him to come and sit near him, to the displeasure of his step mother Queen Kamini.

The King stood and made an announcement "Today, I wish to give my son, the future King of Badshapur, an opportunity which will prepare him for his future responsibilities. " I will be sending him to the Jaadunagari (Magicity) to complete his education and prepare for his destiny – just like our forefathers have done for the last thousand years. The Queen and I will be very sad to see him go but realize that it is for his own good.

Prince Rajvir was shocked and looked towards his father. He noticed the Queen smiling smugly and realized this was her plan of getting him out of the way, to make way for her son, Prince Samir. However he couldn't say anything.

"My son, I know this is very sudden, but we felt it was important that you go immediately as you're already 12 years old and need to complete your formal education" Shaitan Singh the Queen's personal bodyguard will accompany you so that you reach safely. Guruji has already spoken with the Grand Sorcerer and he feels that you should not have any problem settling in. The Hans Vimaana (Swan Drawn Flying Carriage) leaves shortly so you need to catch it else you will not reach in time.

The Queen stood up and took off a ring she was wearing " My son Rajvir, I know you're not my own flesh and blood but I love you like my own – so this magic ring will keep you safe" . As long as you wear it you will never feel hunger or thirst. (What she didn't mention was that the ring was a mini crystal ball and she could keep an eye on him regarding his whereabouts)

The King smiled

"My dear, even I wouldn't have thought of something like that". I also have a parting gift for my dear son – he clapped his hands and a slave stepped forward carrying a golden tray with a long covered object – the king pulled off the silken cloth and there lay a beautiful sword with a jade and diamond handle .

The King said "Behold, the sword of our ancestors, the Sword of Truth – only a hero can heft it".

Prince Rajvir stepped forward and lifted it; it weighed 40 kgs but was light as a feather in his hands.

The King said "This sword can cut through anything from air to hardest granite. The bearer will never feel fear. The specialty of this sword is that all evil beings – demons, ogres, witches, and ghosts, vampires cannot come near you as long as you carry it so never lose sight of it- the sword starts humming the moment something evil is near, This sword can change its size and go from needle length to that of a long spear in a blink of an eye.

Playfully Prince Rajvir pointed it towards where the Queen was sitting, knowing full well she was too far for the sword to react, but suddenly the sword seemed to take a life of its own and started pointing and buzzing softly, so Prince Rajvir sheathed it quickly in its scabbard.

However this didn't go unnoticed by the Queen nor Mandala the court jester who laughed uproariously

" Prince Rajvir, you are only half as mischievous as your father at you age, he would point that sword everywhere, I think it has a got a beehive in it, which explains the buzzing sound"

"That will be all Mandala"said Maharaja Shahvir."Rajvir, the sword will be sent across with the next airmobile and you will receive it on reaching."

Prince Rajvir bowed, but the King hugged and blessed him and escorted him to the Hans Vimaana – (swan drawn – flying carriage) where Guruji was waiting. He frowned when Shaitan Singh stepped forward. Guruji slipped something into his hand – Rajvir sw it was a littleamulet and when he opened it – it contained a leaf." What is this Guruji"? he queried. " This is a magic leaf – when you feel hungry, thirsty or tired – just place it on your tongue and you will immediately be refreshed"

Shaitan Singh was as dumb as he was ugly and Prince Rajvir and Krish delighted in plaguing him especially since he was the Queen's right hand man. A hulking bull of a man with thickset shoulders and close set eyes, big nostrils he reminded them of the mountain apes who would steal into the village at night to raid the orchards and carry away sheep and some said little children too – (according to Dai Maa – especially little children who were naughty and didn't go to bed on time – she would then kiss him and Krish fondly and tuck them into bed).

Guruji and Prince Rajvir climbed onto the Swanmobile and gave instructions to the Swansman to steer the swans towards the East – Prince Rajvir was tempted to take the reins but held back as he was aware that the swans were very temperamental and wouldn't take kindly to a new handler. Big and wild, they were trained from birth to pull the royal families' Airmobiles. Shaitan Singh took up position at the rear which caused the airmobile to tilt due to his weight. The swans had a tougher time of it.

As they flew along Prince Rajvir saw something shining like a huge glass mirror below them, he leaned over and seemed to hear voices calling him – "Rajvir, Rajvir save us, help us".

Suddenly he seemed to hear a female voice ' Rajvir, my son, my dearest son, I miss you, come to me, my child, it is I, your mother"

He leaned over the edge of the Vimaana in a trance and would have fallen over if Guruji hadn't grabbed him .

"Guruji, my mother is calling me, let me go"

"It is not your mother – it is the evil crocodile folk that live in the lake and take people captive as their slaves. They eat the ones who aren't of any use to them. Earlier they used to come out boldly at any time and grab anybody near the lake and take them into it, but since your father's reign this has reduced as he captured their "magic emerald" – desired by all creatures, which, has the power to bring the dead back to life. They are scared that if they come out randomly your father's soldiers posted near the lake will kill them and they wouldn't be able to come back to life, so they behave themselves. They would give anything to capture you as ransom for their "emerald", so never venture near the lake."

Rajvir darted a glance over the side and saw semi saurian shapes with human torsos protruding from the water. He heard grumbling and gnashing of teeth., as they dived back down as they had missed their prize.

As the aerial troupe proceeded, something suddenly whizzed past (a ripe coconut) the airmobile just missing Prince Rajvir. Shaitan Singh grabbed it and broke it open, he reached for a hollow stalk from one of the trees passing below, stuck it in the coconut and offered it to Prince Rajvir, who declined it and smiled his thanks. He Passed it to Guruji who took a long draught from it. Guruji then pulled out his magic staff and waved it in a wide circle calling on Vayudev (wind god) – and suddenly a vortex was formed around them effectively protecting them from any more harm. Further missiles were effectively thwarted from reaching them, thereby fouling the attempts of the mountain apes who were trying to knock them out of the sky. (They believed that the air above their mountain also belonged to them and didn't take kindly to intruders). Shaitan Singh leaned over the side and shouted out a few words in their language and the barrage of missiles stopped for an instant followed by a ripe papaya smashing him in the face and leaving it covered in yellow pulp. Prince Rajbir could barely control his laughter but held out his silk kerchief to Shaitan Singh, who wiped his face.

The swans flew on towards the East and the travelers could see the golden spires of Jadunagari (Magicity) and the city lights twinkling. The city was surrounded by a golden force field which protected the inhabitants from any harm and suspended in thin air on a cloud. The only access was via air. Guruji blew on his conch shell twice and suddenly the aura vanished and the swans headed down to the main city square where the Sorcerers were waiting to meet and greet them. The Sword had also reached and it was handed to Rajvir, who was pleased to receive it. Guruji said he would have it placed in his bedchamber.

Chapter 4 – The Magicity

As Prince Rajvir, Guruji and Shaitan Singh descended from the Hans Airmobile (swan drawn - flying carriage) – the handler blew 3 short tweets on his whistle and the swans took off again heading back to Badshahpur.

The sorcerers were excited to see the Prince and bowed low in welcome – they had all got special gifts for him to help him with his princely progress. Since the trio was tired and hungry they escorted them into the large dining hall lit with lanterns filled with trained glosilk worms that flickered.

These were magical glosilk worms, which were larger than the normal ones and were reared specially to light the lanterns and provide glosilk. The lanterns themselves were enlarged silk cocoons and the glosilk worms flickered away. The sorcerers had a huge need of silk for their robes which was provided by the glosilk worms. The threads too had an incandescent quality and shone and shimmered like a million stars had been woven into the material.

All other material was made of swan down which was soft and could be woven along with spiderweb threads. The butterflies which eventually emerged from the cocoons were huge with varicolored wings and were trained to take the Sorcerers wherever they wished to go when a HansVimaana wasn't available.

The feast was laid out in the main dining hall and there were both royals and commoners who were given admission to the school since knowledge was meant to be shared not restricted. Since Badshapur was the main kingdom – the other princes and princesses came forward to introduce themselves. Prince Rajvir would eventually choose his future wife from among the princesses/girls of noble birth as per tradition. Each diner had a beautifully embroidered rug to sit on – which rose with him/her in case he/she needed to serve himself/herself, saving the bother of having to get up from a chair. The rugs behaved like pets and even lifted a big tassel or two to fan their owners.

Suddenly the chatter died down and there were whispers around that the Grand Sorcerer Shahnawaz was on his way - nobody knew for sure how old the Grand Sorcerer was – legend had it that Grand Sorcerer had lived for thousands of years and could change shape at will so you never knew even if the Grand Sorcerer was sitting right next to you at any time in some different form. Suddenly amid the blowing of bugles the main door opened and a childlike figure walked in accompanied by the other sorcerers and said " Welcome all from far and near, the Grand Sorcerer wishes you a pleasant stay in Mayapur –and will meet you in turn in the Diwaan E Khas (Special Hall) after the meal. In the meanwhile please eat and drink and enjoy your first meal. Prince Rajvir smiled as the dishes were all empty but as he watched the child picked up a wooden dish and spoon and passed it to the first diner saying – " Command it and it will give you what you wish to eat – however choose wisely as you cannot change your choice". The youthful voices rang out with their choice of dish and magically the dish provided it and they served themselves as much as they wanted and passed it on to the next person. Guruji smiled as the dish came to him and said "Pilaf and lamb kebabs", served himself and passed it to Prince Rajvir who commanded " Grilled fish and Tartar sauce". The meal continued till 10 p.m and suddenly the child like figure reappeared and asked if all were done – they were and he clapped his hands and magically the low dining table folded itself up and grew a pair of wings ad flew out of the room.

After dinner the Sorcerers came forward with their gifts a drawstring bag – "this is a magical bag – it could become as large or as small as you want it to be – it blended in with the environment and could not be seen ,until you snap your fingers and it appears, a "looking glass"- through it you can see anything ,anywhere – in all the realms, a magic box – which could speak any language to anybody anywhere in the world from where you were standing. Rajvir bowed and thanked them all but seriously wondered when he would use these gifts – he was to be pleasantly surprised very soon.

It was time to meet the Grand Sorcerer and then head to bed. They trooped towards the Diwaan E Khas and were met by a turbaned slave at the entrance holding a golden book in which an animated quill was noting down names – they held out their right hand and the Quill perked its feathered head and wrote down their name and place of origin in their language. As Prince Rajvir reached, Guruji informed him that only he could go ahead- so he extended his right hand and the quill stopped and seemed confused and then wrote King Rajvir of Badshapur. Prince Rajvir was shocked and turned to see if Guruji was following him but there was nobody so he moved ahead along the passage, confused thoughts swirling through his head – before him was a huge mirror and a voice spoke " Welcome King Rajvir , you have been sent here for a very special purpose and cannot return to Badshapur till your quest is completed. Your father King Shahvir is no more and Queen Kamini has become Regent and her son Prince Samir heir apparent. Shaitan Singh is currently sleeping the "Sleep of the Hundred Years "and will not awake till required. The ring you wear is a looking glass and the Queen is watching you at all times – give it to me" – a pair of beautiful well manicured hands reached out of the mirror and took the ring and plucking a long needle seemingly out of thin air poked the pearl on the ring. Immediately at the other end Queen Kamini's henchman Kalia screamed in pain and held his left eye which started bleeding profusely.

"Curse you Shahnawaz. You will pay for this." shrieked the Queen.

"But what about Avanti and Krish?" asked Rajvir "They have been imprisoned by the Queen – she will not tolerate anybody who is loyal to your cause? Be strong, your people need you. Rest assured when the time is right you will go forward to reclaim what is rightfully yours. Now bide your time. Remember nobody but Guruji and I know what has transpired so do not discuss it – for the walls have ears. Now leave immediately"said Shanawaz.

Suddenly the mirror clouded over and the entire room started spinning and the floor seemed to give way – "Guruji" shouted Rajvir. ""Help me"- as he felt himself falling and everything grew dark.

After what seemed like a few minutes he could hear voices and opened his eyes to find himself lying in a bed which was soft and cottony as a cloud – which is what it actually was. Rajvir was swathed in a cloud duvet which seemed quite dense and comfortable and held together by silken spider web threads. Guruji was standing at his bedside and said "Good Morning Rajvir, you have slept for almost the full day and now it is time for you finish breakfast and to head to the class". "Go and complete your ablutions and follow me". Rajvir got ready in the suit laid out for him, gulped down his breakfast of condensed dewdrops and oatmeal porridge and followed Guruji. Guruji gave him a few scrolls and said. Please go through these, they contain magic mantras which will help you – one is for increasing I n size, the other for decreasing, the third is for reflecting heat and light away from you and the fourth you will read aloud now and find out its use when you need it the most. Guruji felt unwell and told Rajvir to go ahead and he would follow shortly.

Chapter 5 – Flying High

As Rajvir headed down the hall – it felt as though he was walking through a wind tunnel and he seemed to be floating, he looked down and saw he was being carried by a flying rug – with a mind of its own apparently . Guruji chuckled.He held out a golden cruet and said "When you want to fly, sprinkle the magic dust and command the rug "Pari – fly" . If you want to fly faster , tug the tassel on the left," Pari – faster", if you want to slow down, "Pari – slower" and tug the tassel on the right. " What would happen if I tug both tassels at the same time" asked Rajvir – Before Guruji could reply, a rich velvety voice responded " My dear Rajvir, I would rip in half down the middle and you would fall flat on your face" and chuckled deliciously. Guruji admonished the rug "Pari, that is not the way to speak with Rajvir, after all you have been specially commissioned to serve him". "By the gossamer silk thread of my ancestors – I will never fail him "said the rug and flew on at a median pace. Suddenly the rug screeched to a halt – almost tipping Rajvir over. Once you reach the Grand Hall. Guruji said "Go ahead and dip your left hand in the pot on your left – and place your palm on the palm engraving on the side of the door. That is your mode of entry. Nobody else can take your form and enter as you have an unusual palm of 6 fingers unlike others"I will join you shortly.

As he headed towards the educational hall. Rajvir suddenly heard a flutter and felt something alight on his shoulder – a beautiful, silver winged, peregrine falcon which spoke " Rajvir – it is I, Guruji, I cannot accompany you in my true form but since familiars are allowed – will be with you throughout the session. You can call me Vayudoot (Messenger of the Wind)- remember never to address me as Guruji. At night I will revert to my true form. Now you know why I'm in avian form as only sorcerers and students get a flying rug".

Rajvir proceeded as the portal swung open, a sepulchral voice announced his name and the door shut with a thunk. Rajvir found himself in a large amphitheatre with the students seated on their personal rugs and listening intently to the instructor who was facing a large screen. He had a pair of wings which kept on flapping while he spoke and Rajvir could have sworn that his nose looked positively beaky and he had talons grasping the queue stick which he used to point at diagrams on the white board. "Welcome to Flight Class, Rajvir" You're late. Since it's your first day I'm going to let it pass, going forward you will have to pay a penalty for tardiness. Am I clear", he squawked. A couple of students chuckled. Master Swandown swung around aimed a talon and a flash of lightning darted out and struck the students, knocking them over. "That was a low charge, you kids are sitting swans. Why didn't you move, like I taught you?" "Next time, I won't be so kind". The students grimaced and returned to their smoking rugs.

Anyway as I was saying, When I was young, my instructor just threw us off the cloud and we had to flap our wings, and in case we didn't he would let us fall all the way down till we almost crashed and then he would rescue us, take us up all the way and throw us down again. You new generation have it easy, you get a chance to learn from an excellent Professor like me (paused and grinned) and don't have to face what we went through. So as you can see on the board, you need to make sure your wings are well waxed so you can fly – else the feathers will just come off and you will fall to your death. All good sorcerers realize that their magic rugs won't always be there so they have to use their wings and keep them in good working condition. Also make sure your wings can support your weight. So don't go on stuffing your faces with creamy treats (aimed at a plump student who was obviously chewing on a treat) and then find your wings can't hold you up.

Master Swandown had a set of wings for each student – with their names engraved in gold. The wings looked like they had been plucked off angel's backs, and had a life of their own and would have flown away if Master Swandown didn't admonish them sternly " Down, down" like a bunch of unruly children. The students lined up one by one and turned and stretched out their arms and the wings flew over and attached themselves to their backs.

Vayudoot whispered "This is your first test in which you must prove yourself – your wings will find you – be careful" Rajvir stepped forward and surprisingly 2 pairs of wings (1 golden and 1 one plain) flew towards him but before he could help himself a taller, rough looking boy rushed forward, almost knocking him over and grabbed the golden wings, attaching them to his back. Professor Hawkeye squawked indignantly and raised a talon to zap the intruder, but Rajvir naysayed him and took the plain ones.

Professor Swandown stretched out a talon and the huge windows at the rear of the class opened and a gust of wind blew in and animated the wings which started flapping and fluttering to the student's consternation. As one each of the wings started flying independently regardless of the dangling student trying to aright himself/herself. A few of the students took to flying like experts, but others had quite a time trying to get airborne.

Professor Swandown cackled and admonished "I've seen cygnets fly better". "Now observe carefully" – he stretched his wings out behind him in a V shape , checked them and flapped them and then angling them behind him, jumped out of the window. The students followed him in pairs. Rajvir looked out to see them flying in V formation and quickly followed suit along with the last student.

As they proceeded along Master Swandown kept telling them to fly in formation and not fidget.

He said " You kids need to know the Swan Rhyme, so repeat after me"

" *We Swans never falter, we swans never alter, our flight..*

Is right with our wings so silvery bright

We Swans never day dream, we think only about our SWAN TEAM" (Chorus)

We Swans never shirk our work,

It's our trend, we stand by our friend till the very end.

We Swans never day dream, we think only about our SWAN TEAM" (Chorus)

Suddenly there were shadows overhead blocking out the sun rays. Master Swandown squawked and said "Students, watch out, start flying away – we're being observed by the students from our rival school and their Master Hawkeye. He would just love to spoil the training. Head to that big cloud straight ahead please"

As they did they observed that the shadows seemed to be getting larger with every passing minute. The 6 pairs landed on the cloud following Master Swandown's orders. As they stood, gaining their breath, suddenly a group of hawk-feathered shapes descended, almost surrounding them. Their leader was a muscular man with golden hawk feathers and emerald green eyes. He had a supercilious look on his face and smirking said "My dear Swandown, such a pleasure to see you and your troupe. So sorry I disturbed your lesson. Let me know if you need any help whatsoever". All his students cackled at his joke.

Master Swandown retorted "Dear Hawkeye, I have never needed your help, ever since Master Shanawaz asked you to leave Magicity". Master Hawkeye grimaced and replied "You always squawked too much, I challenge you to come out trumps in the Magical Moments Marathon next week. Your team v/s mine, Losers become the winner's slaves for a month. How does that sound?"

Master Swandown smiled and said "Master Shanawaz will decide that – He will speak directly with your head Master Gulnawaz". The Hawk troop flew off as the Swan Troop looked on in dismay. They flapped their wings and headed back to Magicity.

Chapter 6 – Magical Moments Marathon

As the Swan Team reached the classroom and flew through the open window and settled down to work – there was a knock on the door and as it swung open the same childlike figure (from the banquet) appeared with a scroll in its hand. Master Swandown bowed and beckoned – the scroll sprouted a pair of little wings and flew to him- opened and a silvery voice spoke "You are cordially invited to participate in the annual Magical Moments Marathon to be held next week at Middle Land – please honor us with your presence"

Master Swandown said "That rascal Hawkeye knew about this beforehand – that's why he put forth the challenge – will have to speak with the Grand Sorcerer about this"

As the students trooped out and headed towards the dining hall, Vayudoot whispered in Rajvir's ear " "This is your first test – you will have to prove yourself. Kamini has spies everywhere and she will do everything to ensure you fail" You will need to get up 1 hour earlier each morning while still dark and practice your flying as you need to catch up to the other students"

And so going forward Prince Rajvir woke before the sun and went about practicing his flying like an obedient student would follow his master's instructions. Master Swandown commended his efforts to catch up with the class.

The great day dawned and the students woke up early, gulped down their breakfasts and trooped to the Airmobiles to head for the Magical Moment Marathon. They were accompanied by the armed flying guards to avoid any untoward incidents.

Master Swandown instructed them to check their wings once more before the marathon. As they descended towards the venue they could hear the trumpeting of bugles and loud cries of spectators as each team reached the arena. Their hosts had set up an amazing route for the marathon which wound through the Forbidden Forest, the River of Rejection, the Desert of Despair and via the Morbid Mountain through the Tunnel of Terror. Each team would have to procure a trophy from the respective location to prove they had been there. The team was provided with a map to ensure they stuck to the route and didn't wander. They had just 4 hours. Armed guards and wardens would be flying along to ensure that they didn't get into trouble or cheat. A representative of middle land would be present at each spot and would hand over the trophy.

All the teams gathered at the starting point in their allotted positions. They waited and as the bugle blew took off – this was a relay race cum marathon. Rajvir was in last position and he would have to pass through the Tunnel of Terror and exit the mountain. This was difficult as he would have had to manage all 4 trophys. Then he remembered Shanawaz's gift and smiled. Guruji had also taught him a few mantras (spells) which he planned to use at the right time.

All the students went ahead and took up their respective posts.

Rajvir's team comprised the rough boy -Micky (Mikhail) – a Russian Princeling , Jo (Jotaro) – a Japanese Shoguns son and Leo (Leontoh) – an African prince. They were all in the same class and ready for the challenge. The rest of the team comprised Zuma (Montezuma) – a South American Incan Prince, Arthur,an English Prince, Windy "Eagle that Flies Like Wind" – A Native American Chiefs Son, Ferdy (Ferdinand) a Spanish Princeling, Ram (Ramtutmun) – an Egyptian Pharaohs son, Dari (Darien) – a Persian prince and Pericles a Greek princeling.

Mikhail waited at the start line and checked his snowy wings to make sure they were fine – he was headed for the Forbidden forest (The trees were alive and didn't allow intruders in the forest. The students had to figure how to get past them. If anybody tried to force his/her way in the trees would catch them and throw them out or drag them in and never let them leave) Mikhail planned to fly so high above that the trees couldn't catch him. The Hawk, Crow, Eagle teams were already getting set to fly once the whistle was blown

As he took off the wind beneath his wings he looked like a beautiful male swan flying into the sun. As he drew nearer he saw the forbidden forest- the trees seemed lush and green and beckoned invitingly – he seemed to hear them mutter " Coming – come, Going – Go, Staying – don't Stay, Leaving – don't leave" – and then on closer look he saw a number of birds entangled in the branches – those were not birds, those were former winged travelers who had failed to escape the trees and were caught and unable to leave . They called out to Micky – " Help, please help us". As Micky flew higher he realized that if he flew too close to the sun his wings would melt – so he had to maintain a safe distance from the trees and the sun and fly safely- he had already lost a half hour. He was carrying his trusty silver axe to deal with the trees. This was a winged axe and would fly and cut whatever hindered its master. As he flew overhead a creeper shot up and grabbed his leg, but the axe chopped it and so on. The trees screamed at him as their sap blood leaked from the cut ends. The other teams weren't faring too well either.

Rajvir who was watching through the looking glass shouted to Mikhail (using the magic box) a magic mantra (spell) Guruji had taught him and told him to repeat the same after him " Ek ka do – do ka char, yeh kar do baar baar" – (One to two – two to four – do this more n more)- and immediately Micky began to multiply and the sky seemed full of flying Mikhails to the shock of the other teams and the trees below were confused – as they tried to catch each flying Mikhail – he seemed to dissolve and reappear elsewhere. The trees were furious and trying to catch him, their creepers got totally entangled and they were a big muddle. While the mantra persisted – Rajvir shouted out the next mantra – "Teeny Weeny Tiny Tricky – Time to Shrink Micky"and the real Mikhail shrunk so that he slipped between the trees, creepers and landed on the ground right where the Green Goblin Sorcerer was waiting holding up the Golden Leaf Wreath of Wisdom which was the trophy.

Mikhail put it on his head, flew out again, regained his normal size and flew forward. The Crow participant couldn't be seen and would have to be freed later. The Hawk and the Eagle pursued him but he was far ahead and landed on the bank of the River of Rejection and handed the wreath to Jo – who donned it and took off flapping his silver swan wings, over the River of Rejection. The Swan team was in the lead .

The river was like a silver ribbon and was filled with water beings – legend had it that unwanted babies were left by the river bank and they were cared for by the water nymphs. No one had ever gone into its depths.. As Jo flew over the water he saw a pair of hands emerge holding aloft a beautiful samurai sword – like a shaft of lightning. He had seen and envied Rajvir's sword and wished he had one like it. He was tempted to take the sword but as he reached down, another hand emerged from the water and grabbed his obi and tried to pull him under. He reached for his dai katana as he had yet to earn his katana and slashed at the hand. The hand was chopped off and there was a guttural shriek and there emerged a horrible creature from the depths with huge tentacles but the body of a man. This was one of the rivers demon guards, which stopped all intruders. Each tentacle ended in a hand and the chopped hand grew back. The demon tried to grab him and then suddenly it seemed the river was filled with them and Jotaro was surrounded. They grew larger and larger and Jotaro shouted for help. Rajvir observing everything through his looking glass, shouted out another magic mantra. The reverse of the shrinking spell. "Larger than life, amid terror and strife". C'mon Jo time to grow" – Jotaro grew and grew and towered over the demons. They shrieked in fear and ducked down under the water and let him fly onwards.

He returned to normal size, reached the islet in the middle of the river where the Water Witch awaited and she held aloft the same samurai sword which he had seen – Jotaro took it ,bowed his thanks and flew onwards after slinging it over his back between his swan wings.

Jotaro flew onwards beaming like the full moon toward the Desert of Despair where Leontoh awaited. Leontoh flapped his wings and flew over the desert which seemed like a wide sandy sea with nothing visible for miles. The sun beat down and he felt something wet on his back and feared the wax was melting but then he realized it was his sweat – as it dripped and landed on the ground the dust became clay, which started turning into clay soldiers who stood and started shooting arrows as him. Poor Leontoh zigged and zagged to avoid the arrows. to no avail. Flying lower, he drew his Ida and slashed at them but his blade grew dull and under the beating sun he sweated profusely, more and more clay soldiers were formed. Rajvir came to the rescue again and shouted out the reflective spell – "Sunlight super bright – shine now the time is right – Leontoh time to glow". As Leontoh started reflecting the sun's rays he transferred the heat to the clay soldiers which dried up and fell into sand and dust. He flew on and saw the Desert Dwarf seated aboard a huge scarab and holding aloft a silver Spear of Stealth - the next trophy.

He took it, beamed his thanks and flew . He realized that something was following him and there was a shadow blocking out the sun as the eagle team member flew down over him and tried to grab the spear. Leontoh did his best to avoid him but the Eagle team member landed on his back and both fell to the sand – just a few feet away from the finish point where Rajvir awaited on a rock before the Tunnel of Terror. They both scrambled to their feet and started fighting for the 3 trophies. The Eagle team member was larger and poor Leontoh was no match, but he wasn't going to give up without a fight. As the sun beat down on the fighting duo ,the wax melted and their feathers fell off.

Suddenly they heard a hissing sound and found themselves surrounded by 4 varicolored cobras – red, blue, green and yellow which seemed to have risen out of the sand- Rajvir felt " This is Kaminis doing, he couldn't help Leontoh here, else it was forfeit". The Eagle team member grabbed the spear with one hand and grabbed poor Leontoh under his other – dug the butt of the spear into the ground and pole vaulted using the spear straight onto the rock, as the 4 cobras stretched out and tried to bite the airborne pair. They turned around and the cobras had vanished into thin air.

Leontoh thanked the Eagle team member and proferred the spear, saying – you deserve it but he refused saying " You won it, its yours fair and square" Leontoh bowed and said " You have saved my life and now I owe you" The Eagle Team Member smiled, flapped his wings and flew to his Airmobile, knowing he had lost. Rajvir looked around and said " Surprising, I don't see the Hawk team member." He wore the Golden Wreath , slung the sword on his right side, the spear over his back and flew towards the Tunnel of Terror. The tunnel was just like a toothless mouth and a foul smell emitted of rotting matter and gave off a rumbling sound like a dragon was hiding in its depths.. It was the only entrance through Morbid Mountain.

As he flew in – the stench got worse, so he pulled out his silken kerchief and held it to his face. The rotting matter emitted gases which made people hallucinate and not want to leave. Rajvir saw a scene floating in front of him – Avanti and Krish in the royal gardens – Avanti beckoned at him " Come Prince, play with us" and he reached out to touch her hand and she vanished.". He flew on and suddenly he saw a beautiful lady standing before him with tears flowing from her eyes " Rajvir, my son, I miss you " – he felt it was his mother and reached out to her and she reached out as well and hugged him " How tall you have grown" – Suddenly the sword of truth started humming and as he turned it rubbed against his "mother" who cackled and shrieked and tried to have him leave her, but he held on fast and watched her turn into a horrendous hag – " Curse you Rajvir, the sword will kill me, let me go I have done you no harm, I'm just following Kamini's instructions to distract and delay you" – she looked scared and said " Kamini will not spare me for failing her, I must flee" and she started dissolving into dark smoke which vanished.

Rajvir flew to the end of the tunnel and out of the mountain. Suddenly the entire mountain shook and started moving and he realized that it was a sleeping snoring Giant and not a mountain – he had flown complete circle into the giants mouth around his larynx and out again. He was none the worse for it. The Giant gave a toothless grin and held out his hand and on it was a bow and a quiver full of arrows. The last trophy.

Chapter 7 - Sheep in Wolfs Clothing

Rajvir strung it on his back along side the spear and started flying albeit slowly due to the extra weight. As he meandered along he suddenly felt hands grabbing at his wings and pulling the feathers. He twisted and turned and was unable to wrest off the attacker. He realized it was the Hawk team member who was trying to capture the trophies. The wings were torn apart and the feathers floated away. Rajvir felt himself falling like a stone and he thought this was the end. He felt that now it didn't help to be afraid but just relax and meet the earth. So he stretched out his hands and spread his fingers and reached out to the air around him becoming one with it as it rushed past his face and he closed his eyes waiting for the crushing impact.

However he suddenly felt the air rushing past him get slower and slower from shooting needles to light caresses. He heard the shouting of his team members hush and he wondered what had happened – he opened his eyes and saw he was still upright in the air. He wasn't floating nor was he falling – he was seemingly just moving around as though he was on land and then he remembered the 4 th Mantra – it was for levitation. Trust Guruji to know everything.

He opened his eyes and looked around, The mantra when reversed would result in him landing He recited it and he landed with a crash – his team members laughed and helped him to his feet, embraced him and thanked him for his help. They were firm friends from then.

He felt fine and then reached for the trophies – they were all there – touch wood. He turned around .The Hawk team was nowhere to be seen. They had skulked away to their vehicle – they didn't want to be slaves for a month.

Rajvir's team members were furious and swore revenge. As they stepped into the Airmobile they saw the rival teams leave in their respective vehicles. The Hawk team was ahead of them and as usual everything was a competition – their handler trying to race the Swanhandler, the boys got into the spirit of things and the race speeded up with the Hawk handler trying to get them off course. His swan mobile came so close as to nudge them. Mikhail spotted the culprit who had attacked Rajvir, he reached over ,grabbed him and pulled him into the carriage. He squawked for help but before his team could recover, the swans which were slow to respond, suddenly put in a burst of speed and flew ahead and away totally disorienting the hawks, who were left behind. As they reached the Magicity – The handler blew the conch and the aura vanished ,letting them land, late but jubilant that they had won all the trophies. The Hawk team was left empty handed and with no option but to return to Hawksperch.

They hauled the culprit by the scruff of his neck to the Hall of Specialty where the sorcerers awaited and applauded the successful team , bearing the trophies. The Grand Sorcerer Shanawaz – appearing as a hooded figure in a billowing robe, congratulated Rajvir, but he refused to take the praise individually and said it wouldn't have been possible without the Swan team. He started handing out the trophies – the Golden Wreath of Wisdom to Mikhail – so that he would think before he did anything, something he was in dire need of. The Samurai sword of lightning to Jotaro and the Spear of Serenity to Leontoh. They bowed and thanked him. He kept the bow of justness and the arrows of truth.

Shanawaz smiled and said " Spoken like a true prince Rajvir – you're already making your allies who will serve you well in the future.

He turned to the Hawk team member who was cringing in fear – he extended his hand and a bolt of electricity shot out in the form of a noose and circled the Hawkteam members neck and held him aloft like a chicken, he squawked and tried to free himself . " Struggle and you will choke yourself" – do you know whom you dared to place your filthy talons on – he is my student He is like my son. They are all like my children- you touch them and you invite punishment"

The Hawk team member squawked and begged for mercy as the noose tightened. Rajvir held Shanawaz's wrist and the rest of the group shushed themselves to see how the Sorcerer would react. No one had dared to touch him before. Shanawaz smiled and said Rajvir " Let go of my wrist, he deserves what he is getting." Rajvir said "Sir, I beg you, he will never do it again, I'm sure he has learned his lesson". Shanawaz dropped the Hawk like a bag of dirty laundry and turned to Rajvir, smiled and said "You owe me a favor" . Rajvir bowed and said " I owe you my life".

The Hawk team member tried to sidle away but Mikhail stomped on his tail feathers and held him back saying " Scum, you owe Rajvir , your life" . He said " Rajvir ,Sir, I'm sorry, Master Hawkeye forced me to do this, I don't have anybody in this world. If I return to Hawksperch ,they will kill me. May I stay here and serve you throughout my miserable existence – please Sire." The others smiled and said " Sure, we need a Handy Hawk to help around here – dust the rugs, polish our wings, feed the swans, you can do that" " Anything , anything – he said " Just let me live"

Rajvir smiled and said " You can stay here as long as you want as long as you behave yourself. Go rest in the common area – we will discuss your duties tomorrow"

They headed off as it was getting dark. Vayudoot said " Smart move Rajvir, now you have one of their members on your side – you can find out what they're upto anytime" Rajvir responded pensively " Why not, sounds like a good idea. I'm very tired and will discuss this with you tomorrow" Vayudoot responded "Sure, sure – you rest, you have worked very hard today. I have made a special energy drink for you and left it by your bedside. Have a sip and you will feel better. I hope the trophies have been kept in a safe place" "Not now – they're lying in the common area – will hand them over to Grand Sorcerer Shanawaz tomorrow". Vayudoot responded "The Hawk Team member is there, you don't think he will try something" – "No – I'm sure he has learned his lesson- I'm very tired – will sleep now"- Rajvir yawned and headed to the sleeping chamber – Vayudoot responded " Sleep tight Rajvir, don't let the bugs bite " and chuckled at his little ditty. Rajvir took up his sword which was lying on his bed and it hummed softly as though to let him know it was there. Rajvir smiled and said " Sword, take a break, you're perpetually humming, No wonder Mandala compared you to a beehive. There is nothing evil here

Rajvir yawned again, laid it near his bedside table and it hummed away – like a little lullaby. In no time he was asleep.

Chapter 8 - The Enemy Within

After ensuring Rajvir was asleep, Vayudoot fluttered down the darkened hallways to the common room. The entire place was quiet as a tomb – nobody was around. Even the winged guards had turned in their wings for the night and were nodding off peacefully.

Vayudoot flew through the open door of the common room and heard a soft snoring .The Hawk team member was snuggled in his cloud coverlet and fast asleep. He looked around and the trophies lay where the boys had left them. "Tsk Tsk, so careless of them, let me put them in safe keeping so they don't get damaged".

" So considerate of you Vayudoot or maybe that isn't your real name" said a voice and Rajvir stepped out from behind a cloud column - accompanied by Jotaro, Leontoh, and Mikhail, who was already furious at having his sleep disturbed and was brandishing his axe.

" Rajvir, I mean Prince Rajvir, it is I – why are you speaking like that, you know I'm really your Guruji"- said Vayudoot.

"No, you're not ". I was suspicious from Day 1 when you said you had to change your form and appear in your true form at night and not to tell anybody. You also said that you didn't have a flying rug, which is surprising since all sorcerers have one and Guruji was also a former student of the school. Hence he could command Pari. Why all the secrecy? I then realized that you had an ulterior motive and didn't want to be recognized. Also you always made an appearance and gave advice when my sword wasn't there except for a little while ago when you followed me to my bedchamber to check if I was really asleep and the sword sensed it. You weren't there when I was participating in the Marathon until the end, unlike Guruji who would never leave my side, because you were informing the Hawkteam about our whereabouts. That's why they knew when to attack me just as I had finished the marathon. And lastly you took an inordinate interest in the trophies – which made me realize that you have a hidden motive."

"And he knows you're not his Guruji because I am he" said a disembodied voice and with a flash of light Guruji appeared, Rajvir ran and hugged him". "You thought that the magic potion you slipped into the coconut would have its effect on me but understand that it is for normal human beings, not sorcerers. I informed Shanawaz and we wanted to see what your long term plan was hence we didn't inform Rajvir. I was always present invisibly and had already shared the magic mantras in the beginning so he could use them during the marathon and had warned him about shape shifters. So now you can show Rajvir who you really are?'

"Well well well, smartly played Rajvir & Guruji – but not that smart – said Vayudoot aka Shaitan Singh in his true form of a tall horned hairy demon with bat wings. I could have thrown you to the crocodile people from the Airmobile. I waited too long to finish you off – as I wanted the magical trophies first. But anyway , no regrets, no time like now to finish you off . Kamini will be pleased and will reward me well. You and Krish took me lightly and I know what fun you made of me. Now you pay – with your life – and he pointed a clawed hand and a rope of red energy shot out but Guruji chanted a mantra and a blue energy bolt countered it . Guruji was old and couldn't hold off the demon for long as the red energy started increasing in length and spreading out, it attacked the others as well reaching out to catch Mikhails axe and then his throat and likewise with Jotaro and his dai katana. The next tentacle of energy grabbed for Rajvir. Suddenly the Hawk team member stepped in front of him and blocked the energy, which seemed to have no effect on him due to the hawk feathers which acted like an armor. Rajvir grabbed his sword and slashed at the energy rope and cut it in half but it grew back again and again like it had a life of its own.

"Enough – you dare to step on sanctified space" thundered a voice – Grand Sorcerer Shanawaz appeared accompanied by Leontoh. :You have woken from your sleep and you must return forever and he pointed a finger and a vortex of green energy opened and enveloped the demon in a whirlpool and sucked him in , while he did his best to escape – as he vanished he shouted out " Kamini will not spare you for what you have done. You will pay dearly".

Rajvir hugged Guruji who was recovering from the shock and had to sit on a cloud bench. Grand Sorcerer Shanawaz smiled and said "Well done,,old friend" and patted Guruji's shoulder (who was gasping for breath)

"I'm not as strong as I used to be" he said. Rajvir thanked the Hawk Team Member – who bowed his head.

"Tell me why the feathers counter the energy?" asked Rajvir " Thousands of years ago the Hawk leader signed an unbreakable pact with the demon lord for protection – as a result this energy has no effect on us – however what I have done now is an act of defiance and punishable. I'm afraid for my life" responded the Hawk Team member.

"As long as you stay in this magic bastion you are safe" said Shanawaz- "Do not be afraid"

"I am going to work a magic mantra of protection around all of you which will protect you when you step out – this will be centered in these magic amulets. So at whatever cost you must not lose them – if you do then the dark powers can take control of you"

The Beginning of The End

The boys gathered around Guruji – he looked pale – it was as though the energy was drawn out of him.

"He is infected", said Shanawaz – " that wasn't an ordinary energy bolt – it is like a magnet it draws out magical energy from the host like a parasite and channels it back to Kamini through her familiars – We have just found one familiar, there are many more around the world. Killing them all off will take time. Kamini has absorbed energy for hundreds of years and she is very strong – it is all centered in the breast plate she wears. Now that she has tapped into Guruji she knows our whereabouts. He will have to be placed in a secluded area before she finds us." Suddenly Guruji laughed and spoke in a high pitched female voice"Good job Shanawaz, but not good enough – you will realize this when I enter the Magicity to take what is rightfully mine".

"No Kamini, you will never be successful in that, not as long as I am Grand Sorcerer".

"We shall see about that" – she responded and laughed again eerily.

"We all have to be extra careful –Kamini isn't afraid anymore and as each day passes her powers will get stronger and stronger – she is planning to attack; this is just the **Beginning of the End.** Either Good or Evil will prevail. If Kamini succeeds we will enter a Dark Age, no one who contests her will survive and her rule will be so terrible that only the dead will be happy. Even now she uses the Dark Arts to contact her minions around the world to prepare for the Great Battle.

Rajvir, you cannot return to Badshapur till the time is right.

All of you follow me to the High Library, we will have to consult the scrolls and see what the oracle has in store for us.

All the boys were awed – the rest of the Swan team had also gathered and they all followed the Grand Sorcerer to the inner sanctum, the entrance being the Mirror.

As they passed through the Mirror –they found themselves in a hall of mirrors and were shocked and surprised as they looked through each at different parts of the world- their home countries or so it seemed.

Is this real or Maya (Illusion) – asked Rajvir . The Grand Sorcerer smiled and said " It is as real as you or I are.

They moved forward and reached a circular table with a crystal disc embedded in it . The Grand Sorcerer clapped his hands and the disc emerged and started rotating slowly . "Tell us oh Oracle, what Rajvir needs to do next, what do you see " asked Shanawaz

The Grand Sorcerer went into a trance and the oracle spoke through him

"I see Rajvir in a land far away – it is very cold and everywhere there is ice and snow – he is fighting a battle with an old enemy – the Winter Wizard – but he also has a friend to help him".

"Rajvir, be careful, all is not what it seems. BEWARE. Friends will turn foes"

The Grand Sorcerer shook and came out of the trance and looked around.

" What did the Oracle say" – he asked Rajvir, who repeated what had transpired.

"Hmm – that means you will have to go on a journey - to the North to fight the Winter Wizard. Who will accompany Rajvir on his quest ?

" I will" – responded Mikhail, before the others could respond – " Well said" – you are the chosen one." responded Shanawaz.

"The Winter Wizard is attacking our borders and taking away our children as slaves- she has to be stopped" said Mikhail.

"Exactly – he is very powerful – he draws his power from the cold – destroy that and he is vulnerable". said Shanawaz

"How do we do that" asked Rajvir ?

"You have to make him face the Eye of the Sun" said Shanawaz and it has to be done during the day.

"How do I get it?" asked Rajvir .

The journey will be difficult – travel to the Land of the Rising Sun with Jotaro and pluck it from the Dragon King who holds it.

Once you get it you and Mikhail can proceed to the North.......

Glossary

Andher Kothri – Dark Rooms

Daii Maa – Nurse mother

Guruji – Teacher

Kaalia – Black One

Kamini – Evil one (Female)

Magarmacch Log – Crocodile Folk

Rajvir – The Bravest in the Kingdom

Shahvir – Brave King

Shahnawaz –Nurturer of Kings

Shaitan Singh – Devilion

Suryadev – Sun God

Vayudev –Wind God

Vayudoot – Messenger of the Wind

Author's Write Up: The Author Llessur, has from a young age, had an avid interest in fantasy and magic and has always wanted to write stories for young boys and girls, teaching them not to stifle their inner creativity, leading a humdrum rat race existence but rather aim for the stars. He has travelled extensively overseas and has lived in the US & Australia. He currently resides in the metropolis of Mumbai, India with his family and is a Corporate Trainer and professional storyteller. He also likes sketching and would probably be managing the illustrations for the book and book cover.

www.ingramcontent.com/pod-product-compliance
Lightning Source LLC
Chambersburg PA
CBHW022038150726
47990CB00004B/1516